# Rockets

## STAN THE DOG

# Stan and the
# Golden Goals

WHOOOSH!

# Scoular Anderson

A & C Black • London

# For Alexander

**Rockets series:**
**CROOK CATCHERS** - Karen Wallace & Judy Brown
**HAUNTED MOUSE** - Dee Shulman
**LITTLE T** - Frank Rodgers
**MOTLEY'S CREW** - Margaret Ryan & Margaret Chamberlain
**MR CROC** - Frank Rodgers
**MRS MAGIC** - Wendy Smith
**MY FUNNY FAMILY** - Colin West
**ROVER** - Chris Powling & Scoular Anderson
**SILLY SAUSAGE** - Michaela Morgan & Dee Shulman
**SPACE TWINS** - Wendy Smith
**STAN THE DOG** - Scoular Anderson
**WIZARD'S BOY** - Scoular Anderson

First paperback edition 2003
First published 2002 by A & C Black Publishers Ltd
37 Soho Square, London W1D 3QZ
www.acblack.com

Text and illustrations copyright © 2002 Scoular Anderson

The right of Scoular Anderson to be identified as author
and illustrator of this work has been asserted by him
in accordance with the Copyright, Designs and Patents Act 1988.

ISBN 0-7136-6145-3

A CIP catalogue record for this book is available
from the British Library.

A & C Black uses paper produced with elemental
chlorine-free pulp, harvested from managed sustainable forests.

Printed and bound by G. Z. Printek, Bilbao, Spain.

# First Helping

Stan loved chasing things. At the top
of his list were cats.

But there was
a big problem
with cats. They
were very good
at getting out
of reach.

3

There were rabbits at the far end of
the park. Stan liked scaring them.

But like the cats, they soon got out
of reach. It wasn't very fair.

Sometimes, Stan
tried to go after
them, but he always
got into trouble
for covering himself
in bits of park.

Chasing sticks was better because he always caught up with them. Stick-chasing usually happened when all his family went into the park. The one Stan called Canopener never threw sticks.

Crumble couldn't throw sticks.

5

Bigbelly threw sticks when he was in the mood. His aim wasn't very good and the sticks usually ended up in the middle of the pond...

...or up a tree.

The best stick-thrower was Handout.

Stan liked chasing balls best of all. He loved the way there was an extra chase when the ball bounced up in the air.

Handout liked football so he was always kicking a ball around the back garden.

Stan sometimes acted as goalie.

Being such a good goalie, Stan was really excited about the football trials. Every day, he jumped up on the kitchen stool to check the calendar.

He was quite sure he'd get on the team to play the big match against Lairdberry Juniors. He might have been a dog but that didn't really matter. He had *talent*.

# Second Helping

The day of the trials arrived. Handout came home from school and had a snack. Stan took up his usual place under the table.

But Handout didn't give Stan a handout.

Stan wandered through to the
sitting room.

He leapt up onto the sofa and shoved
the cushions out of the way.

He found a few biscuit crumbs...

...a couple of crisps...

...and half a bar of chocolate.

Finally, he tried the armchairs, too.
He only found a small, plastic box.

Stan had to wait for Handout to get
ready. Just to make sure he wasn't
forgotten, Stan lay by the front door.

Stan got a shock when Handout arrived at last.

Then Bigbelly arrived.

Stan was
horrified.

He was desperate to get out of the door.

# Third Helping

Mr MacTackel the trainer was on the pitch.

The match started. Stan took a great interest in the game.

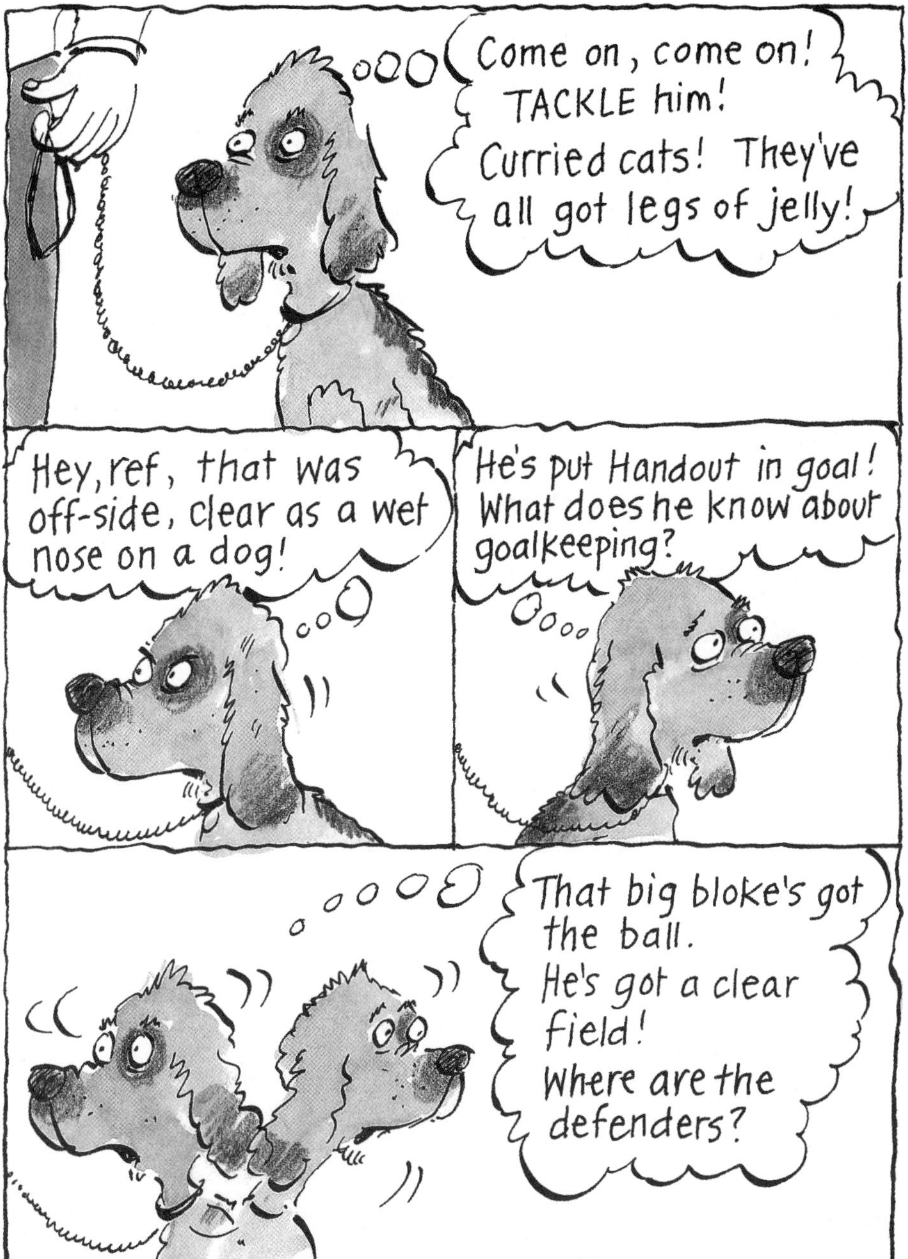

Stan couldn't bear it any longer. He
dived forward and the lead slipped out
of Bigbelly's hand.

The boy with the ball was lining up his shot...

...but in three bounds, Stan was in the goalmouth.

The ball flew...

GDUNK!

...and Stan dived.

WHOOOSH!

The ball shot up...

...Stan shot back...

...the goalposts collapsed.

Handout was wild.

Bigbelly went to apologise to Mr
MacTackel.

Mr MacTackel
blew the final
whistle. Everyone
went into the hut
for refreshments.
Handout was still
furious with Stan.

Bigbelly tied Stan
up with the lead.

# Fourth Helping

Stan sat and wondered what was
happening inside the hut.

At that moment, a snack fell out of the
sky.

Then the owner of the French bread
came out of the sky, too.

The bread was just a bit big for the crow
to pick up easily. Stan thought he was in
with a chance.

But each time Stan moved forward...

...the crow managed to jump just out of Stan's reach.

Round and round the pitch they went.

Just as Stan made a final leap, the crow managed to get the bread into its beak and fly off.

Stan was in for more trouble when everyone came out of the hut.

Bigbelly had tied Stan up to the white-lining machine that was used to paint the lines on the pitch.

As Stan had chased the crow, he had dragged the white-lining machine behind him. The pitch was now covered in white lines.

Mr MacTackel was very good-natured about it.

Handout *wasn't* good-natured about it.

On the way home, he refused to have anything to do with Stan.

# Fifth Helping

Handout had been picked to play for the team, but not in goal. For the rest of the week, after school, he practised in the back garden.

This isn't fair.

Stan wasn't allowed to play. He had to watch from inside the kitchen as Handout still wasn't speaking to him.

Handout grew grumpier as the day of the match drew nearer. On Saturday morning he laid out his kit neatly on his bed.

Stan went to wish him good luck but Handout still didn't want to know.

At last the time came for Handout to go to the football pitch.

Down at the pitch, the visiting team arrived in a minibus.

Their trainer looked at the rickety old goalposts.

He stared at the lumpy, bumpy, soggy pitch covered in white marks.

He turned up
his nose at the hut.

At last the big game got started.
Lairdberry Firsts were soon three
goals up.

Stan had to watch the game from inside the car.

Stan wound down a window...

...squeezed out of the car...

...and was soon racing home at great speed.

I hope I get there before the other two leave!

The back door was still open and
nobody saw him go in.

He dug out
what he was
looking for
from behind
the chair
cushion.

Then he ran back to the football pitch
with it.

Hope I'm
in time!

The game had stopped for injury time.
Handout was gasping and wheezing.

At that moment
an inhaler appeared!

Handout inhaled deeply, after a few
moments, he was able to play again.
Right away, he scored a goal.

But it was the only goal his team got.
Spratston Cubs lost one goal to five.

# Sixth Helping

Just as everyone was heading home,
another minibus pulled up by the pitch.
A woman jumped out and came across
to Bigbelly.

Excuse me, is this your dog?

She showed them a card.

Di Mulligan
producer
ACE-ENTERTAINMENT
COMPANY

We're filming for a TV programme called Paws for Prizes.

It's about animals who do clever things or help their owners.

Di Mulligan took a photo out of her folder.

Handout changed back into his football
boots to kick balls to Stan for the camera.

# Seventh Helping

A few weeks later, the family sat down round the TV to watch 'Paws for Prizes'.

They were just in time.

Then there were lots of shots of Stan as a goalie. He didn't let a single ball through.

Stan won, of course. His family decided to use the money to improve Spratston Cubs' football pitch.

Handout tied his football shirt round
Stan's neck.

Stan couldn't stop wagging his tail.

They gave Stan a special tea.

Then the family went out to celebrate in a restaurant. Stan didn't mind being left at home.